COLLECT-A-PET

My cute

PUPPY

Written by Helen Anderton

make
believe
ideas

Reading together

This book is an ideal first reader for your child, combining simple words and sentences with beautiful photos of puppies. Here are some of the many ways you can help your child with their early steps in reading.

Encourage your child to:

- Look at and explore the detail in the pictures.
- Sound out the letters in each word.
- Read and repeat each short sentence.

Look at the pictures

Make the most of each page by talking about the pictures and spotting key words. Here are some questions you can use to discuss each page as you go along:

- Do you like this puppy?
- If so, what do you like about it?
- What would it feel like to touch?
- How would you take care of it?

Look at rhymes

Many of the sentences in this book are simple rhymes. Encourage your child to recognize rhyming words. Try asking the following questions:

- What does this word say?
- Can you find a word that rhymes with it?
- Look at the ending of two words that rhyme. Are they spelled the same? For example, "small" and "ball," "chase" and "place."

Test understanding

It is one thing to understand the meaning of individual words, but you need to check that your child understands the facts in the text.

- Play "spot the mistake." Read the text as your child looks at the words with you, but make an obvious mistake to see if he or she has understood. Ask your child to correct you and provide the right word.
- After reading the facts, close the book and make up questions to ask your child.
- Ask your child whether a fact is true or false.
- Provide your child with three answers to a question and ask him or her to pick the correct one.

Puppy quiz

At the end of the book, there is a simple quiz. Ask the questions and see if your child can remember the right answers from the text. If not, encourage him or her to look up the answers.

Key words

These pages provide practice with very common words used in the context of the book. Read the sentences with your child and encourage him or her to make up more sentences using the key words listed around the border.

Picture dictionary

A picture dictionary page illustrates the things you need for taking care of a puppy.

Watch me grow

When I'm born, I'm very small.
I like to curl up in a ball.
But soon I'll grow —
just wait and see!
Will you be best
friends with me?

nose

DID YOU KNOW?

Puppies don't open their eyes until they are nine days old.

eye

ear

5

Mommy and me

I love lying on my tummy,
snuggling up beside my mommy.
My nose is soft and my fur is like silk.
I like to drink a lot of milk.

silky fur

DID YOU KNOW?
Out of the five senses,
the first one that a puppy
develops is the sense of touch.

Mommy

Whoops!

As I grow, I learn to crawl.
I try to stand,
but WHOOPS I fall!
I tumble down
and get back up.
What a wobbly
little pup!

paw

DID YOU KNOW?
Puppies begin learning to walk when they are two weeks old.

leg

Woof, woof!

Now that I'm bigger, I love to play
with my littermates every day.
We yelp and flop and roll around
near our mommy on the ground.

DID YOU KNOW?
A puppy's heart beats between 70 and 120 times a minute — much faster than your heart!

littermate

Time to eat

I like dog food for my lunch.
I chew and bite and
munch and CRUNCH!
But what I love
the BEST to eat
is my tasty
doggy treat!

bowl

DID YOU KNOW?

When puppies begin teething, they chew toys to help ease the pain in their gums.

Play with me

I've got so much energy –
I love it when you play with me!
Playing FETCH is best of all;
I run to get things when you call.

14

DID YOU KNOW?
Puppies bark to show you they are excited or to tell you they are hungry.

toy

Let's go outside

I love racing through the trees
and chasing butterflies and bees.
I stick my nose deep in the ground.
WOOF! Look what I've just found!

leash

nose

DID YOU KNOW?

When it is three weeks old,
a puppy's sense of smell is 1,000
times better than yours!

Zzzzzzzz!

When I'm tired from playing chase,
I like to find a quiet place.
I curl up in a cozy heap,
and with a YAWN, I fall asleep.

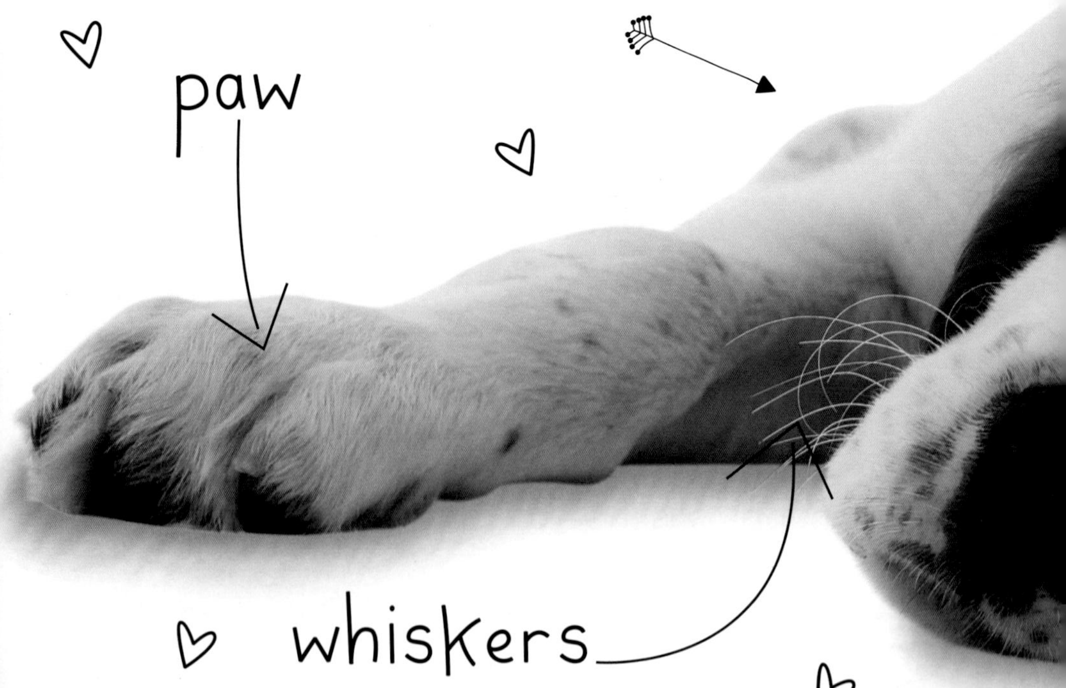

paw

whiskers

DID YOU KNOW?

Puppies need 14–16 hours of sleep every day, which means they spend more than half their time napping!

Teach me tricks

You teach me lots of fun new tricks.
I catch the ball and bring back sticks.
I lift my paw and shake your hand,
or sit up very tall and grand.

tail

DID YOU KNOW?
Puppies can learn simple tricks when they are only 10 weeks old.

stick

collar

Playing with my ball

Hard balls, soft balls, big or small,
I love playing with them all!
Best of all are balls that bounce:
throw them high and
watch me pounce!

DID YOU KNOW?
It might take a puppy a few months to learn how to catch a ball in its mouth.

ball

23

Let's visit the vet

It's time for a checkup at the vet.
He helps to keep me a healthy pet.
He measures both my weight and size,
then checks my ears,
and mouth and eyes.

DID YOU KNOW?

Puppies' coats need regular brushing to keep them healthy.

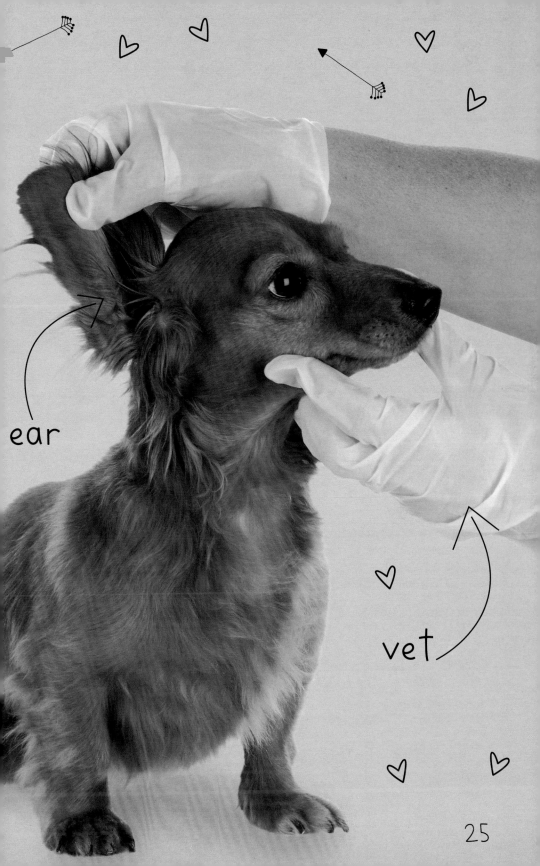

ear

vet

25

All grown up

Look at me!
I'm big and tall.
I run all day
and chase my ball.

I know I might
look all grown up,
but in my heart,
I'm still your pup.

26

DID YOU KNOW?

Most puppies reach their full size when they are one year old.

Puppy quiz

How much do you know about me?

1. How old are puppies when they open their eyes?

They are nine days old.

2. How old are puppies when they learn to walk?

They are two weeks old.

3. Why do puppies bark?

They bark to show you they are excited or to tell you they are hungry.

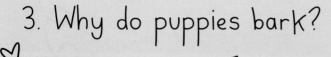

4. How many hours of sleep do puppies need every day?

They need to sleep for 14 hours.

5. How old are puppies when they can learn simple tricks?

They can be just 10 weeks old.

6. What do puppies' coats need to keep them healthy?

They need regular brushing.

7. How old are most puppies when they reach their full size?

They are one year old.

Key words

Here are some key words used in context. Help your child to use other words from the border in simple sentences.

I have soft fur.

I chase **my** ball.

on ♡ at ♡ for ♡ a ♡ he ♡ is ♡ go

I love going **for** walks.

Look at our spotted coats.

Let's **play** catch!

I chew treats **and** bones.

you ◁ are ◁ this ◁ going ◁ they ◁ away ◁ play

big ♡ dog ♡ the ♡ day ♡ get can ♡

Picture dictionary

ball

basket

blanket

bowl

brush

collar

doghouse

leash

toy